10.50

10/1/2020

I0659750

Night of the
TODDLERS

WRITTEN BY TOMMY DONBAVAND
ILLUSTRATED BY FRAN AND DAVID BRYLEWSKI

LONDON·SYDNEY

Franklin Watts
First published in Great Britain in 2016 by The Watts Publishing Group

Credits
Executive Editor: Adrian Cole
Design Manager: Peter Scoulding
Cover Designer: Cathryn Gilbert
Illustrators: Fran and David Brylewski

HB ISBN 978 1 4451 4685 0
PB ISBN 978 1 4451 4686 7
Library ebook ISBN 978 1 4451 4687 4

Printed in China

MIX
Paper from
responsible sources
FSC
www.fsc.org   FSC® C104740

Franklin Watts
An imprint of
Hachette Children's Group
Part of The Watts Publishing Group
Carmelite House
50 Victoria Embankment
London EC4Y 0DZ

An Hachette UK Company
www.hachette.co.uk

www.franklinwatts.co.uk

Contents

Chapter One:
You Beauty

Professor Nigella Troppy popped the cap on her test tube, and poured a single drop of green fluid into the dish in front of her. She watched as the chemical reacted with the liquid already in there, fizzing slightly.

Could this be it? Had she finally succeeded where everyone else had failed? There was only one way to find out...

She removed one of her safety gloves, and tipped a glob of the cream onto the wrinkled skin on the back of her hand. With trembling fingers, she began to massage it in. Her flesh began to tingle, then tighten — and then it became younger!

She was a 59-year-old woman — with the hand of a 20-year-old! And she could feel the effects spreading throughout her body.

She pulled a mirror from her pocket
and gazed at her reflection. Her skin was
smooth, her eyes bright and her body full
of youthful energy.

After twenty years of tireless testing, her Born Again cream finally worked!

The door to the lab swung open and Professor Fanton Smooth eased into the room. As usual, he was smartly dressed and wearing a gleaming white lab coat. Even the You Beauty company pass that hung around his neck was sparkling.

Nigella fluttered her suddenly lengthy eyelashes at him.

"Oh, I'm sorry, my dear!" crooned Professor Smooth. "I was looking for my colleague, Professor Troppy..."

Nigella's youthful cheeks blushed hot pink. "Fanton," she said. "It's me, Nigella — just a much younger version. My Born Again cream works!"

Fanton gasped. "What? You're old Troppy Knickers?"

"I am," Nigella said. "And I'll definitely be promoted to Chief Scientist for this!" She closed her eyes and sighed happily. "A huge pay rise, company sports car, state-of-the-art new laboratory. They'll all be mine!"

Fanton cleared his throat. "Ah, well that's what I was coming to tell you, old girl," he said. "You see it turns out the You Beauty bosses really liked my 'Tastes of the Sea' toothpaste. They've just promoted me to Chief Scientist..."

Professor Troppy's right eye twitched.

"What? That's not fair!" she roared. "I've been working on my youth cream for twenty years — all you've done is given a few women fishy breath!"

Fanton shrugged. "That's the beauty business for you, old bean. Now, I'm off to the top floor to pick up the keys for my new lab, and have a browse through a sports car catalogue."

"But ... but...!"

"Lovely working with you, my dear. Cheerio!"

Professor Smooth was almost at the door when Nigella had her idea. "I say, Fanton..." she said. "I really don't want to let petty jealousy come between us."

Professor Smooth stopped with his fingers on the door handle. "Delighted to hear it," he beamed. "The best scientist won, and all that!"

"I couldn't agree more!" exclaimed Nigella. "You're exactly what this company needs: a Chief Scientist with charm, intelligence and youthful good looks..."

"If only," Fanton said with a sigh. "Sadly, my better years are long behind me."

Nigella waved a dish in her rival's direction. "Not necessarily..."

Fanton's eyes grew as he pictured himself as a much younger man, speeding along in his brand-new car. "You'd really let me try that stuff?"

"Of course!" replied Nigella, slinking over to her workbench. She lifted the test tube again, but instead of a single drop, she poured all of its contents into the remaining Born Again cream.

"I'll even give it a bit of a boost for you..."

Chapter Two:
Born Again

Bobby Savage wandered from market stall to market stall, his hands stuffed into his pockets, and his brain whirring. His mum had to be the hardest person in the entire universe to buy a birthday present for!

His thoughts were interrupted as his twin sister, Gail, appeared at his side. "Found anything?" she asked.

Bobby shook his head. "Not so far. How about you?"

"There's a really nice make-up set on the stall over there," Gail said, pointing. "But we haven't got enough for it."

She pulled a twenty pound note from her pocket. They'd been saving the change from their dinner money for over a month to get this much. It was vital they spent it on just the right gift.

"Well, I'm out of ideas," Bobby admitted.

"I might not be," said Gail with a smile. Grabbing her brother's hand, she led him to the far side of the market square where a new stall had been set up.

Behind the table stood a beautiful young woman in a white coat. She was busy setting out a number of large tubs, each with a handwritten label on the side.

"Born Again cream?" said Bobby, reading aloud. "What does it do?"

"It makes you younger!" promised the woman. "And it's just £19.99!"

"Perfect!" beamed Gail. "We'll take one!"

"Hang on," said Bobby, grabbing his sister's wrist. "How do we know it works?"

"Because I invented Born Again cream myself!" replied the woman. "You won't be able to tell — but I'm really 59 years old."

"And she's a proper scientist!" Gail hissed, gesturing to the company pass that hung around the woman's neck. "Look — You Beauty."

"Ignore that!" snapped the woman, tearing off the pass. "I don't work there anymore! They don't appreciate genius."

She tossed the pass to a young boy of around two or three playing behind her. The toddler instantly stuffed it into his mouth and began to chew.

"Aww! He's cute!" said Gail, waving to the child. "Is that your son?"

"What? Fanton?" spat the woman. "Never in a million years would I — erm ... I mean, no, he's not my son. I'm his aunt. Yes, that's it. His Auntie Nigella."

The toddler smiled up at Professor Troppy and held his hand out towards her. "Don't touch me!" the scientist shivered. "I don't know how easily that stuff spreads through contact yet!"

"What stuff?" asked Bobby. "Do you mean your Born Again cream?"

"No, of course not!" said the Professor quickly. "He, er … he had a doughnut earlier and I'm allergic to … holes. Now, do you want to buy my cream, or not?"

"We do!" smiled Gail, handing over the twenty pound note. Professor Troppy took it carefully and grinned. "The first of many…" she whispered to herself.

Chapter Three:
Happy Birthday

It was raining heavily by the time Bobby and Gail arrived home. They glanced up at the large windows at the front of the house. The curtains were open, and they could see flashing lights illuminating the interior. Loud disco music pumped out.

"The birthday party's already started," said Gail. "We're late."

"It doesn't matter," said Bobby. "We weren't invited anyway."

Inside the house, the music was deafening. The twins kicked off their wet shoes and knocked on the door to the lounge. A moment later, it was opened by a middle-aged woman squeezed into a shimmering pink dress three sizes too small.

"What do you want?" she slurred, taking a swig from the cocktail in her hand. "Don't you know isth my burrfday?"

"We know, Mum!" said Bobby with a smile. "That's why we got you this..."

Gail handed over the tub of Born Again cream. "Hope you like it!"

Mrs Savage squinted at the handwritten label, put down her glass, then flipped the lid off the pot and sniffed at the cream inside. "What's this stuff?" she demanded.

"It's new," said Gail. "We bought it from the scientist who invented it."

"It makes you younger!" added Bobby.

Mrs Savage scooped a dollop of the cream onto her fingers, and began to smear it onto her bare arm.

Another face appeared at the door. It was a man in a tight-fitting designer shirt. "Where've you two been?" he demanded. "I had to carry all the booze in myself! Nearly broke my back!"

"Sorry, Dad," said Bobby. "We were out getting Mum a present..."

Mr Savage rubbed his hand up and down his wife's arm. His palm came away sticky. "Yuck!" he said, wiping the goo on his trousers. "What's that grot?"

"Youth cream," smiled Gail.

Mr Savage looked his wife up and down. "I think she's a bit past that stuff," he said, matter-of-factly. The comment earned him a slap from his wife.

As his dad rubbed his sore cheek, Bobby peered around him to a table heaving with party snacks, and felt his stomach rumble. "Can we get some sausage rolls?"

"No, you can't!" snapped Mr Savage. "Do you think I slaved over the phone ordering all that stuff from the caterers, just to waste it on a couple of stinking kids like you?"

"No, Dad," said Bobby, lowering his gaze. "Sorry, Dad."

Gail held her arms wide. "Happy birthday, Mum!"

Suddenly, the music changed to an up-beat rock anthem. "Oh, thissss is my faffourite!" cried Mrs Savage, tossing the tub of cream onto a nearby armchair.

Then she and her husband disappeared back inside the room and slammed the door.

"Come on," said Bobby.

The twins made themselves some toast, and took it up to their bedroom.

Lying back on her bare mattress, Gail sighed. "I don't think Mum liked her present," she said quietly.

"Of course she did," Bobby assured her.

"She's just busy making sure everyone has a good time."

"Yeah," said Gail, pulling the thin sheet over her shoulders.

Despite the loud music and laughter from downstairs, Bobby fell asleep instantly — only for Gail to wake him in the early hours.

"What's wrong?" he asked.

"Ssshh! I think I can hear a baby crying."

"What?" said Bobby, sitting up and rubbing his eyes. The music had stopped, and the house was silent. "You must have been dreaming. Go back to—"

Then they both heard the wail of an unhappy young child.

"Quick!" hissed Gail.

The pair crept down the stairs and stopped at the lounge door. "It's coming from in there!" mouthed Bobby.

The two children cautiously opened the door and froze. There, stumbling around in the middle of the room, were half a dozen moaning toddlers.

Chapter Four:
New Queen

Bobby took a step backwards. "Whoah!" he said. "What's going on? Where are Mum and Dad?"

"There!" cried Gail. Bobby followed her gaze. In the corner of the room, chewing on a mobile phone, was a sour-faced young girl, wrapped in a baggy pink dress. A boy wearing a man's designer shirt sat next to her, scribbling on the wall with an expensive lipstick.

"That's impossible!" Bobby said, picking his way between the other children.

Gail stopped him. "Don't touch them!" she commanded, climbing onto the table and kicking the remaining food to the floor. The crying toddlers stopped blubbing and crawled over to feast on the spilled party snacks. "And don't let them touch you!"

Bobby quickly clambered up beside his sister. "Why not?"

"It's that cream," said Gail, pointing to the open tub of Born Again that still sat on the armchair where their mum had tossed it. "Mum and Dad both rubbed it onto their skin, remember? It's made them younger. Much younger!"

"But, what about everyone else?" Bobby asked.

Gail shrugged. "Maybe the effects can be transferred by touch?"

Bobby nodded. "This is the first time I've been grateful for Mum and Dad never hugging us."

"We have to stop the effect from

spreading," Gail said.

"Too late for that," said Bobby, looking out of the window.

Outside, wandering around under the streetlights, was a pack of around thirty young children. They toddled along together in various states of undress.

The twins could just about hear their muffled cries through the glass.

"Mama!"

"Where's my teddy?"

"I wanna biscuit..."

"Of course," sighed Gail. "The Professor sold more than just one tub. People took them home, like we did, or into where they work. The whole of London could be infected — or worse."

"Maybe there's something about it on the news," Bobby suggested.

Grabbing the remote, he switched on the TV and flicked through the channels until the familiar 24-hour news show appeared. But, instead of the regular newsreader,

a three-year-old boy sat behind the
reporter's desk, swamped by a large jacket.

"I did a wee-wee!" he said.

"It's everywhere!" said Bobby. "The
effect of the cream, I mean. Not the wee-
wee." He was about to hit the OFF switch
when a new face appeared on the screen.

It was an adult face.

An adult face that the twins recognised.

"Look!" hissed Gail. "It's her — the woman who sold us the youth cream!"

On the TV, Professor Nigella Troppy draped a red, fur-lined robe over her shoulders, and sat down on a throne. Behind her, the walls were covered with large oil-paintings, hanging in golden frames.

"I recognise that place!" hissed Gail. "It's Buckingham Palace!"

"Girls and boys of Great Britain!" Nigella announced. "I say girls and boys because, by now, there will be no ladies and gentlemen left! You're all toddlers!"

"Not all of us," Bobby muttered.

"I realise that broadcasting my big day to a nation of infants is a bit of a silly idea," Nigella continued. "But I wanted to record it for history."

She leaned round and swung the camera down to show a handful of toddlers playing happily on the plush carpet with a pair of corgis. The young boy named Fanton was with them.

"As you can see, the royal family's all here for the big occasion!" said Nigella, tilting the camera up again to show her face, only this time she was wearing a crown.

"Ta-da!" she said, sneering directly into the camera. "Toddlers of Great Britain, bow down before me — Queen Nigella the First!"

"If I had to list the things I never

expected to see today, that would be number one," said Gail.

The screen hissed once more, then returned to the 24-hour news channel, where the newsreader was sitting in his chair, his face red and straining. "And there's number two!" cried Bobby, snatching up the remote and turning off the TV.

He sat on the edge of the couch and sighed. "What do we do?"

"Simple," said Gail. "We pay a visit to the new Queen!"

Chapter Five:
Noisy City

Despite the lack of traffic, London was as noisy as ever. But, instead of the beeping of horns and revving of car engines, the streets were filled with the sound of crying and wailing toddlers.

The little children were everywhere: spilling out of doorways, wandering aimlessly along pavements or curled up fast asleep.

Gail tried to tune out the sound of their

cries, focusing instead on the hum of rubber tyres as she and her brother raced down the lamp-lit road.

"I still feel bad about this," admitted Bobby.

"Relax!" said Gail. "We've only borrowed these bikes. We'll take them back once this is all over."

Swerving to avoid a pack of tottering toddlers, Bobby pedalled harder to catch up with his sister.

"Who's going to feed them?" he asked.

"Feed who?"

"Everyone in Britain!" said Bobby. "Right now, there are around 65 million mouths about to get very hungry. And, even if we could find food for them all — then there's an even bigger, stinkier problem to deal with at the other end..."

"Let's just concentrate on finding a way to fix things," said Gail.

BONG! BONG! BONG!

The sound of Big Ben echoed out as the children cycled past the Houses of Parliament. Then came another noise — the roar of a car engine approaching.

"Quick!" hissed Gail, jumping off her bike. "Hide!"

Bobby dumped his own borrowed bike and crouched with his sister behind a bus stop. They watched as a sleek, red sports car came racing along the street, headlights blazing, and zoomed past them towards Trafalgar Square.

"That was her!" exclaimed Bobby. "Queen Nigella!"

Gail nodded. "This way."

The children stood...

...to find a horde of toddlers swarming down the street towards them.

"HUGS!" they moaned, arms outstretched. "HUGS!"

"There are thousands of them!" cried Bobby.

"They must have been attracted by the sound of the car!" said Gail. "Now we can't get back to the bikes!"

The pair ran towards Trafalgar Square, dodging smaller groups of terrifying tots.

Reaching the square, the children skidded

to a halt. It was packed with pottering pre-schoolers.

Bobby glanced back at the waddling wave of whippersnappers approaching from behind. "We're trapped!" he croaked.

"Not for long!" said Gail, grabbing Bobby's shoulders. "Drop to your knees!"

"What?"

"Just copy me!"

Bobby quickly knelt down, his face splitting into a wide grin as Gail started to shuffle forwards on her own. She had her arms held out in front of her, and was chanting, "HUGS! HUGS!"

Bobby did the same, adding "I need a poo-poo!" in a squeaky voice.

The toddlers paid no attention to them.

"Brilliant!" hissed Bobby. "They think we're big toddlers. But how are we going to get all the way to the Palace?"

"Look!" said Gail, pointing.

Parked on the opposite side of the road was an ice-cream van.

"Oh, no!" said Bobby. "Borrowing bikes is one thing, but stealing that..."

"We're not going to steal it," said Gail. "Watch..."

Shuffling across to the open door, Gail hauled herself up into the van and began to flick switches. Eventually, the speakers on the roof began to blast out a warbling version of the song "Greensleeves".

Every single toddler in central London paused for a moment, then swarmed as one towards the tinkling tune.

"ICE CREAM! ICE CREAM!"

"That should keep them busy for a while," said Gail as she jumped back down.

"You're a genius!" grinned Bobby.

Together, the twins stood and raced along The Mall towards Buckingham Palace.

Chapter Six:
Last Laugh

The gates of Buckingham Palace were flung wide open, and the red sports car the twins had seen earlier was abandoned outside.

"Looks like someone is home," said Gail, nodding towards a doorway.

"Come on, the guards are all taking a nap."

Inside, they quickly followed the sound of crying to the throne room, where they found the group of babies that had once been the royal family. They were crawling about, waving politely to each other.

"One has soiled one's nappy!" said a little boy with large ears.

"Who are you?" snapped a voice. The twins looked up to see Professor Troppy enter, carrying an ice bucket filled to the brim with food. "And why aren't you toddlers like everyone else?"

"Let's just say this is the one time we're lucky we don't get hugs," said Gail.

"They're the lucky ones!" exclaimed Nigella, pointing out of the window. "I've given them the gift of youth! And I took what I deserved. A posh new home, an expensive car, and you won't believe the size of the pay rise I've given myself!"

"You turned people into toddlers against their will," Bobby pointed out. "Now they're tired, cold and hungry."

Nigella shrugged. "Hardly my fault if they can't look after themselves..."

"It's totally your fault!" cried Gail. "Turn them all back, right now!"

"Sorry," said Nigella, twirling her robes

with a flourish. "Can't be done."

"What do you mean?" demanded Gail.

"There's no way to reverse my Born Again cream," said the Professor flatly. "Once you're young, you stay that way."

"You didn't make a cure?" said Bobby.

"Of course not! Who wants a beauty cream that makes you look older?" Nigella's eyes narrowed as she stared down at the twins. "You've lost, not-so-little ones!" she sneered. "And now I just have to decide what to do with you. I could smother you in Born Again cream and take you back to your terrible twos, but I think I may just keep you here as my servants…"

Bobby and Gail shared a nervous glance

as Queen Nigella the First began to approach them ... until she caught her foot in the fur-lined hem of her robes and toppled forwards, crashing to the ground.

"HAHAHAHA!" giggled the toddlers.

Then — FLASH! They were suddenly all adults again!

The twins found themselves staring at several semi-naked members of the royal household. The royals leapt behind the nearest sofa to hide.

Then, Queen Elizabeth II stood from where she had been feeding the corgis the crusts from her cucumber sandwiches.

"Your Majesty!" said Gail with a curtsey.

"Your real Majesty!" said Bobby, bowing.

"WHAT!" screeched Nigella, clambering to her feet. Two re-grown security guards grabbed her by the arms and held her. "Who did this?"

"I did!" said a voice. A well-dressed man stepped out from behind the throne.

"Fanton!" croaked Nigella.

"Do you really think I was promoted to Chief Scientist for inventing toothpaste that tastes like fish?" he scoffed. "No, Nigella — I was there as a spy, watching you. And I made sure there was a way to reverse the process, in case you ever decided to infect the population with your evil paste. All the toddlers need to do is laugh, and they'll be back to their normal selves again."

"But... But I worked for decades on that youth cream!" Nigella sobbed. "Just look at me! I'm beautiful again!"

"I shouldn't worry," said Professor Smooth. "Even if you never laugh again, you'll be old and wrinkled by the time you get out of prison! Take her away."

As Nigella Troppy was led away by the guards, Queen Elizabeth opened her arms wide and hugged both Gail and Bobby tightly.

"You have both done very well indeed!" she said. "But there is still a lot of work to be done. So, I'd like to make you an offer..."

Chapter Seven: Fresh Start

Bobby and Gail sank back onto the soft twin beds in their new room. They'd been given the best decorated suite in the whole of Buckingham Palace.

"I'm exhausted!" said Bobby.

"Me too," agreed Gail. "That was the longest game of peek-a-boo ever!"

The twins had spent the last seven days on the balcony at the front of the palace, entertaining bus-load after bus-load of tired and hungry toddlers as they arrived from all over Great Britain.

It didn't take long to make the little ones laugh, after which there was a FLASH, and a crowd of confused adults were suddenly standing in their place. Royal staff were ready and waiting to explain what had happened, and to hand out dressing gowns where needed.

After a week of hard work as the Queen's official Happiness Patrol, the children had turned almost the entire population back to its old self.

Gail sat up on the edge of her bed. "Let's try with those two again," she said, gesturing to a door on the far side of the room. "You know, thinking back — I can't recall either of them ever laughing."

"Neither can I," said Bobby. "But this new idea might work..."

Gail opened the door and stepped into the next room, where two toddlers sat on the floor, looking glum. "Hello, Mum! Hello, Dad!" she said with a grin.

"Time for fun!" beamed Bobby as he

rushed in, carrying a bunch of flowers.

Suddenly, Gail stuck out her foot and tripped her brother over, sending him crashing to the floor. When Bobby sat up again, he had tulips in his ears, and two large daisies over his eyes.

"Thanks a *bunch*!" he moaned to his sister.

The two young toddlers sat in stunned silence for a second, then they turned to look at each other — and they smiled.

THE END